AF107806

A Line Inwards

Admer Balingan

Ukiyoto Publishing

All global publishing rights are held by

Ukiyoto Publishing

Published in 2025

Content Copyright © Admer Balingan

ISBN 9789370093928

*All rights reserved.
No part of this publication may be reproduced,
transmitted, or stored in a retrieval system, in any
form by any means, electronic, mechanical,
photocopying, recording or otherwise, without the
prior permission of the publisher.*

The moral rights of the authors have been asserted.

*This book is sold subject to the condition that it shall
not by way of trade or otherwise, be lent, resold, hired
out or otherwise circulated, without the publisher's
prior consent, in any form of binding or cover other
than that in which it is published.*

www.ukiyoto.com

To my teachers—

for every work that came through you and unfolded in ways loving.

Contents

Everyday Reveries.	1
Lines Back to the Heart	2
Finding Stardust in the Ordinary	4
Horrors at Twilight	6
To Bask in a Few Dawns from Now	7
The Sweet Paradox of Empty Cages	9
The Quiet Art of Just Being Here	11
A Few Illuminations Before Dawn	13
The Ground Beneath the Leap	15
Magnifying the Small Joys	17
Little Evidence of Living	18
Carrying the Lightness of June	21
One Day, I'll Grow My Own	22
I'm living for this kind of feeling,	23
On Idleness	25
Ode to Nanay Rosa	27
Lessons from My Window	29

Lights, Stories, and a Line to the Heart.	**31**
Breaking Ceilings	33
The Basics You Taught Me	35
Someone Who Sits Through the Storms	36
The Language of Places	37
A Hundred Countries Away	38
Currents of the Heart.	**41**
Teach Me Who I Am	43
Soft Entrances	44
To Grieve on the Living	45
About the Author	47

Everyday Reveries.

Lines Back to the Heart

Here's where I end up after a long promenade. I keep coming back to this place when I think about a not-too-pricey and simple escape. The sky is a lovely mix of gray and orange, the air is calm, and so are the trees. There's not much to see today, or hear, or do; it's almost the same. Cars are passing by, people coming in and out, tables standing still, chairs remaining tucked in, the room not so packed, ceiling flowers are still ceiling flowers, a woman receiving orders, a guy serving them... I don't know, but

I think there's solace in the sameness of things when you recognize them as they come to you, to name the feelings of a memory, and organize them when all's tangled up and strange in the vastness of things.

You know when you are out in the vast, you can always draw a line inwards and always go back to what's familiar at heart—one that may be secluded, or abstract, or somewhere only you know the way in and out. People or art or poetry; it's not necessary to learn or look at them differently. What's necessary is you look at them and keep looking at them, and see that there's nothing strange to work on. It's done already.

The way they are is the way they are. And it's not strange. What's strange is when you think there's still a lot of work to do.

- At a quiet café tucked away somewhere in Indangan, Davao City.

Finding Stardust in the Ordinary

I don't know what feeling good is all about, except for the moments spent alone with a good book and coffee, and listening to Van's "Into the Mystic."

I don't know it except for going on long walks around both familiar and unfamiliar places, engaging in conversations with both friends and strangers. It's about seeing Mogu's tail wagging when he sees me back home, admiring fairy artworks online, and losing myself in all things mystic, cottagecore, and tarot. It's stumbling upon places out of sudden curiosity and crying over poignant scenes from series, but also experiencing moments of laughter.

A lot has been happening lately—mostly rough—and being able to identify what touches the heart, what makes it burst with macro stardust, is something that keeps everything manageable for me. It keeps me anchored to magic everywhere, in many forms—in quiet moments, in flowers, in swaying branches, in mosquito bites, in rendezvous, in spontaneity, in the different hues of the sky, and even in cheese-covered fingers...

    right here.

Horrors at Twilight

So much had happened in the past few hours, days... and these were some things that one wouldn't be blamed for grieving over. My heart breaks in ways of splinters as I hear distressing stories within and beyond the regions, especially in my very home in Surigao.

Everything seems very uncertain at this time, and as much as I want to think more about it—the horrors in every dawn and twilight, the overwhelming thoughts that keep me awake at night—I understand how much in this world is beyond my understanding and control. And sometimes, it's just better to let things be. Having that thought is comforting in a way, thinking less, and allowing my grounds to rest for a while. Just letting the flowers fester in most of the spaces, including the ones fresh from cracks and cuts.

I mean, today is no metaphor for beautiful. I mean, today, I just need to be one of the flowers.

Written during a time of consecutive earthquakes in December 2023, which deeply affected regions including Caraga.

To Bask in a Few Dawns from Now

I've been missing a lot of calls lately and receiving messages that I don't have the chance to respond to. I hope they know that I appreciate them for reaching out, whatever the reasons may be, and understand that there are days when I can't even get up and carry myself to face another day. That it's also breaking me to be like this.

Things have just become so much heavier that I can't even do simple tasks like laundry, going outside for a walk, cooking for myself, or functioning normally like other people do. I hope they understand that there are days when I'm not comfortable speaking to people and that I sometimes lose the strength to share what my life has been like lately because it always takes a huge amount of energy to come up with descriptions. I'm afraid I won't be fully present in the conversation, that I'll run out of words to say, and won't know how to keep it going.

But I hope they understand that I miss talking to them, too. I miss hearing their voices and listening to what they want to share about their lives with me—whether it's about their recent achievements and how they're going to celebrate them or their plans for the next five days.

I hope they understand I've been having down moments and hard days, too, where all I can do is either stay in bed or sit quietly in a corner, listening more than talking. But Heaven knows I'm trying to emerge from it, however slow.

I'm trying to function again like I used to—to dance in the rhythm of the wind again, like flowers and trees do. To stand in front of the world again, more excited. However slow. However slow.

The Sweet Paradox of Empty Cages

Days ago, I went out of my room out of reflex; there were no particular reasons why. I didn't have a checklist of what I needed to do, like interesting things to complete or groundbreaking types of things; I just went out without plans and with mere empty hands.

For a moment there, I stood under the canopy of trees, surrounded by the quiet richness of greens. For a moment there, birds started to make an angry noise around the branches, almost sounding like a new anger poem to write about. For a moment there, the wind started to whisper to the leaves, almost sounding like a new secret conversation worth keeping in my notes.

For a moment there, I saw an empty cage, and it almost spoke to me of how life can be a sweet paradox sometimes; you can look at it as an object to scare the birds or to hold them captive, but you can also look at it as a space birds have outgrown because they might have grown bigger wings and voices that they don't fit in there anymore. But it doesn't necessarily mean flying, nor are birds bound to unfold their wings provocatively.

Moving outside doesn't have to have reasons. This is no longer about birds. I realize there is so much to see, to write about, to fall for, to be angry about, to feel with your heart, to remember lovingly, without having to see it clearly, at first. The same way I'm writing this without a reason to begin it in the first place. I just write everything down, and everything... everything just flows.

The Quiet Art of Just Being Here

So, you see, I don't have much to offer. I don't carry enough weight with me wherever I go to break ground. I don't astound the flowers. I don't mesmerize the trees and everything in the ecosystem that I share my presence with. I'm not remarkable like the greatest poems ever written, or paintings ever painted, or poets ever lived. I don't echo like the fused voices of the activists, nor am I as stirring and pointed as the critics'. I just flow like how dry autumn leaves do, falling freely to the ground you never know is even there.

But I'm here. I'm still here, with a beating heart, with enchanted eyes pointing skyward, with bones rooted in the ground breathing the way poems do in aloneness, the way tales spring from a muted territory, the way art comes to life from the lifelessness of the world.

This is what being here means for me; it's witnessing how every work that comes through me unfolds in ways loving, implausible, and unhurried. And it may not always cause the ground to break or make grand enhancements of the mundane—I see a way to exist as I am, to create in synchrony with my hands, to frolic, to sing happy tunes even for small reasons. Like seeing the Bengal clock vine bloom for the first time.

That kind of happy tune.

A Few Illuminations Before Dawn

There's something about a coffee shop and the scent of freshly brewed coffee with a good book that takes me away from the surface. It's something I can't say no to—a kind that beckons me to sit in quiet, to listen closely to the vibration of the world inside, the poetry and music in it that my heart dances in rhyme with.

It always feels like returning home, where the child in me can frolic while a huge part of that world is growing up and expanding so massively that I get lost in its strangeness sometimes. I stand in front of it small and unprepared, trying my hardest to learn from scratch, only to end up more confused.

There are still more bent roads now. Some unexpected cars crashing down, some lamplights in the morning that I never thought would be both brighter and more blinding than they are at night.

There's so much newness in it, so much to grapple with, to catch and fit in small hands just so I can tell myself I've done it all. But I often forget to fill my hands with enough memories. And sometimes, beautiful memories are made in silent minutes like this—in slow moments, sitting in front of sunlit windows, in the first sip of warm coffee, in the first bite of cookie bread, in the smile and kindness of a barista, in the magnificence of Antoine de Saint-Exupéry, and listening to mellow Backstreet Boys songs played on a loop.

I want to live for moments like this. I want to witness them in the world and understand that we're supposed to live as familiar as children, not grow as strange as adults.

The Ground Beneath the Leap

Life outside writing has been filled with so much newness. There are things I find quite a marvel and, at the same time, scary. I'm not sure if I've done the right thing or if I've just had to do it, regardless of whether it's right or not. All I know is that I must go out there, despite both holding back and pushing forward.

I feel such a huge paradox—wanting to root in muteness, yet also wanting to grow loudly and visibly by trying new things outside of my *normals* and exposing myself to worlds I never thought I could blend into, however different they are from where I stitch stars among dreams and poems among flowers.

Stepping outside has been a huge leap of faith, without knowing what ground will define my form when I land—or if there is even a ground to land on in the first place. There is a frank lostness in between. There are twisted lines I wish I hadn't crossed and others I'm thankful I did. There are more pitfalls than smooth roads, and there is breaking even before I realize it. But I'll always come home to this: to rest, heal, and recenter between poetry and writing. I'll always come home to where I am my least fine-tuned and most quiet, raw, whole, awake, touched, alive.

This is poetry putting rhythm back into my heart. And this is me dancing along with it.

Magnifying the Small Joys

I always get fascinated by how, in such utter randomness, I find my heart in an inrush of beautiful energy. Just this morning, I wasn't used to waking up early because I stay up at night most of the time writing stuff, daydreaming, and crying over things that have been bloody hard and consuming for me lately. I spend long hours in bed, but I still often wake up with squeezed bones, feeling as though elephants ran over me the whole time I was asleep.

But with the surge of something strange, yet familiar, I started to look at things in a different, good light. I hadn't picked up the broom in a long while, but this morning I did. I hadn't opened my window and door in a long while, but this morning I did, letting the wind and sunbeams in. I hadn't listened to Taylor in a long while, but this morning I played her 1989 version, blasting it at full volume while singing along, dancing, and cleaning my tiny room.

It felt like working my way out of the black hole, magnifying these little ways, and I find it a beautiful thing—to sing my heart out, open up, jump out of bed—and how, in such utter randomness, I find my way through life again.

Little Evidence of Living

There's a small pile of papers on my desk. It's been there for weeks. Every time I see it, I tell myself I should sort through it—throw away what's unnecessary, file what's important. But today, I didn't. Today, I just sat there and looked at it.

At first, it felt strange—just sitting and staring at a mess. I've always thought clutter was something to fix. But as I looked closer, I realized it wasn't just a pile of papers. There was a receipt from a café where I'd spent a quiet afternoon, its edges slightly frayed. There was also a photocard I got just a few days ago—a prized find after days of trying. I'd been visiting Dunkin branches at odd hours, even in the middle of the night, hoping it would finally be available.

And then there were loose sheets of paper with my handwriting, little fragments of thoughts I must have written down in a hurry. Some of them I didn't even recognize anymore, but they still carried the energy of a moment I'd been excited about.

The longer I looked, the less messy it all seemed. The café receipt reminded me of a warm moment by myself, sipping coffee and watching the world go by. The photocard made me smile again, a little victory that felt sweeter for all the effort it took to find. Even the random notes felt alive, like tiny pieces of a life being lived in bits and bursts.

I didn't clean it up. I didn't move a single thing. I just let it be, and somehow, that felt right.

I didn't even make my usual Earl Grey today. Instead, I remembered a Spanish latte I'd stashed in the fridge earlier this week. I poured it over ice, its creamy sweetness feeling like the perfect pause in a day where nothing needed to be rushed.

After a sip of latte, I opened Fleur I recently discovered in my effort to bring some order into my life. If I wasn't going to fix the clutter on my desk just yet, at least I could try organizing something else.

Then I turned to my reading list on Notion. It was as cluttered as my desk - titles I'd added on a whim, books I'd forgotten about, and a few I'd already finished but never marked as complete. I didn't overhaul it, just moved a few of my favorites to the top. It felt good to make even a small adjustment, like clearing a tiny path forward.

It's funny how I always feel the need to clean, to organize, to make things neat and presentable. But sitting with the clutter today, I realized it wasn't just stuff. It was a collection of small, scattered evidence that I had been here, that I had lived through these moments, and that they mattered, even if only to me.

I finished the last sip of my latte, the cup now empty, and the pile still full. Maybe I'll sort through it tomorrow. Or maybe it will stay, quietly growing, holding more of the moments I haven't yet made sense of.

Carrying the Lightness of June

    I always take a moment to pause when I pass by this heap of bougainvillea on my way from work to the boarding house. It's lovely to witness its magnificence, the way it sways and is cradled by the wind in the quiet afternoon of June. I feel a part of me is touched by the blessing that comes with its soul-filling presence, a sanctuary I can turn to when there's been a draining void amid a long day. It always reminds me to go gently, kindly, lightly. And in whatever I do, I'm humbled to see the beauty in carrying this lightness forward. I feel uplifted.

    I feel the touch of magic that springs from it.

One Day, I'll Grow My Own

It used to be here—the bougainvillea, which I loved so much and looked forward to seeing again every time I went to and from work, was cut down. It saddens me how things suddenly disappear without warning. The impermanence is scary; one day, it's still there, and the next day, it's gone.

I grieve in my thoughts because nobody really knows how one person feels a bit lighter seeing it alive and blooming—how the mere presence of a bougainvillea can make one person, or even someone else passing by, feel glad seeing or touching it. Who knows? I don't own it, and I do acknowledge that even things we own, borrow, or marvel at have their own time to slip through the cracks of our fingers, no matter how much we don't want them to.

It was my little joy; I cherished every feeling its brief presence brought to my heart. One day, I will have to grow my own bougainvillea... and let it flourish.

I'm living for this kind of feeling,

and I don't want to let it die like January embers. I'm in all ways disarmed in these silent minutes and the poetry that becomes known only when lived. I want to feel it and let it linger more in the miracle this moment carries. Bask in the quietude and forget about the monotony of the highway or the laundry list of creative briefs. This is magic I could never articulate well enough myself. This stirs me, softens me, and heals the little broken go-getter in me.

The past few days were a blur of late nights, tear-stained pillows, and playlists around the how-to-stay-afloat narrative on repeat. Each movie marathon offered a fleeting escape only to be replaced by the crushing weight of my own thoughts. Hozier describes it as *"a coming of squall."*

(Cut to) I found a book today called *Long Night Stands with Lonely, Lonely Boys*. I never expected it to become my instant favorite, but its pages drew me in. Learning about the author added another layer to the experience, connecting me to their words in a way I didn't expect.

Life is this, I guess. One found in the slow moments, unexpected detours, those precious instances where you step back and recenter. This is about surrendering to the quiet moments; even the tough ones can sometimes feel necessary for a fresh restart and unending beginnings. As Hozier puts it:

"And just knowing / That everything will end / Should not change our plans / When we begin again."

Maybe it was a dream, or perhaps just the gentle passage of time, but whatever this is, I woke up feeling a touch lighter.

On Idleness

I've been digesting a lot of things lately to the point of idleness—at work and outside of it. Personal matters, adulting, valid IDs, crossroads, and... how to stay alive.

Oftentimes, I stick to my bed longer; it feels like a territory I can't escape from. I like to put things on hold. Dilly-dally. I watch an unhealthy amount of movies based on random snippets I've seen online that got me curious. I've become so immobile that even my monthly stats recap on Strava doesn't inspire me anymore to go back to walking or running. When I attempt to read, I think about writing. And when I write, I find myself staring at the I-beam on Google Docs, as if it were a dead end. I've got so much heavy writing to do, but it feels like I'm at a loss for words every time.

It was a year ago when I remember writing every day like a mantra. I started my day with it—through poems, prayers, wishful thinking, affirmations, and reminders. I even revisited drafts and continued writing them, though I'm far from finishing them. It was a year ago when it was easier to finish writing a page and keep writing more pages, and more that I didn't realize were adding up to thousands of words. But presently, each day I die thinking about writing but barely write. Even in moments when I feel I need to write, I can't. Every day feels like a graveyard of unsaid words, and I lament in the ugliest ways.

I don't know how to clear the blockages or step out of the idleness. I guess I just need to deal with it and meet everything as it is. I want to go back to writing, to my heart, to what feels softest within myself. Sometimes, maybe it's not about coming up with a piece every day; maybe it's about revisiting old pieces or some of the online writers whose words speak frankly to my heart, like Benj's. Maybe it's taking my indoor plants outside to water and let them soak in the sunbeams. Maybe it's redecorating my room, repositioning the crochet plants I received from a high school classmate, calling a friend for help, or eating out with high school friends I haven't seen in a long time.

I've read a lot of Pizarnik too and attempted to write but ended up sounding like her. Maybe I just need to try again after so many failed attempts.

And maybe... I just need to permit myself to write, regardless of what it looks like.

Ode to Nanay Rosa

Sunday mornings always take me back to the sound of Nanay Rosa's voice. You'd hear her long before you'd see her. "Puto!" she'd call, carrying her transparent plastic container, its lid fogged up from the warm puto inside.

I remember how Mama would head out with a smile, a few coins jingling softly in her hand. Moments later, she'd return with a plateful of soft, warm puto, placing it on the table before heading to the *abuhan*, where she'd light a fire using dried wood and coconut husks.

She'd heat water in our old *takure*, the one that had darkened over time from years of use. The spout had a slight dent, the handle worn smooth, like it had shared in every morning of our lives. Mama would toss in some roasted rice once the water boiled, stirring it slowly until the air filled with that familiar toasty scent.

That smell, mixed with the warmth of the puto, was enough to make the whole house feel alive. We'd sit around the table, dipping the soft puto into the hot coffee Mama poured straight from the *takure*. I remember how the coffee would leave a trace of bitterness on the puto, but somehow, that made it taste even better.

They say some things change, and some things stay the same. And maybe that's true. Life has changed a lot since then. But hearing Nanay Rosa call out in the morning still feels like home. It's like a little piece of my childhood that never really went away.

Even now, years later, Nanay Rosa still walks the streets, still calls out just as loudly, still carries her familiar *tupperware* packed with puto. Every time I hear her voice, it feels like stepping back into those quiet mornings of my childhood—Mama by the door, the smell of roasted rice coffee, and the feeling that, somehow, everything was in its right place.

And on mornings like this, when I hear her voice again, I'm reminded of how something as simple as soft puto and strong coffee can hold so much love, so many memories. It makes me pause, take a breath, and feel grateful—for Mama, for those mornings, and for the little things that make life beautiful.

Lessons from My Window

There's a line from Mary Oliver that always stays with me: *"Let me keep company always with those who say, 'Look!' and laugh in astonishment, and bow their heads."*

It's such a simple thought, but it captures something profound about how I want to live. And oddly enough, I think about it most when I'm sitting by my window, watching the sky.

There's something about the sky that feels like it's always whispering, "Look!" It doesn't shout or demand attention, but it's impossible to ignore. Every moment, it changes—soft mornings bathed in pinks and oranges, midday skies stretching wide and endless, and sunsets that seem to set the world on fire with their colours. Even at night, when the world quiets down, the stars come out like tiny sparks of wonder, asking us to notice them, to marvel.

What I love about the sky is how it reminds me to slow down. It doesn't wait for us to appreciate it—it just is. But when you do stop and look, it feels like the most generous gift. It's humbling. It makes you want to laugh at how small and fleeting everything is and bow your head in gratitude for the chance to witness it at all.

And maybe that's why Mary Oliver's words resonate so much. To live a life full of wonder, you need to surround yourself with people who are willing to look—to pause, notice, and be amazed. The kind of people who see a brilliant sunset or a sky full of clouds and can't help but point it out, who remind you that there's joy in simply being alive to see it.

The view from my window has become my little teacher in astonishment. It doesn't matter what kind of day I'm having—there's always a moment when the sky seems to nudge me, as if to say, *"Look at this. Isn't it incredible?"* And I find myself nodding back, grateful for the reminder.

So, here's what I hope for: to keep company with the sky, with those who notice it, and with all the small miracles we often take for granted. To laugh in astonishment, even at the ordinary, and bow my head in gratitude for it all.

After all, what else is there to do with life, if not to live it wide-eyed and full of wonder?

Lights, Stories, and a Line to the Heart.

A Line Inwards

Breaking Ceilings

I've been so skeptical about what I want and need in life. I've been living a free-falling life without meeting a certain ground. You can imagine how free, reckless, stubborn, or magnified I can be. No walls ensnare me. No, I don't fit in the boxes. But when you came into the picture, for the first time, I found out what being shut in a completely foreign, yet familiar corner feels like. I've known the sound when you reach the ground, falling hard. It's scary, irreclaimable, and… beautiful at the same time.

You drew that sound like a history on my heart that I could trace with stern gentleness, so as not to break a part of you. I understand more clearly the person I've been and the one I'm becoming because of you. I might've been lost between the lines, but you came to me as an answer and reminded me of my ground and all the possibilities that can spring from it.

Despite the heft of history you shoulder and the legacy you've been wounding yourself to carry and march upwards for the world to see, there you are, rewriting history and coming up with a fresh page without margins. There you are, writing your story and leaving no spaces unfilled. There you are, healing all the voices you toned down for the world to listen to you. And I listen to you, in every voice and every version of you.

You've become the sound that vibrates and that I can dance with in my dreams, when I wake up, when I breathe, every day. I'll immortalize this sound as that blunt kiss one New Year's Eve, that dance amidst the statues, and us breaking the ceilings.

We're moving forward somewhere—no history, no color, no power, no authority—can dictate what this love will look like.

- Inspired by the movie *Red, White & Royal Blue (2023),* directed by Matthew Lopez.

The Basics You Taught Me

I don't know what it's like to look at and deal with life without learning the basics you taught me—but necessary ones. What I learned throughout the years of my solitude, living in terror and uncertainty, and reading the signs of nature to survive would never suffice to move forward in the real world outside the marsh. You came to me with a harmless intention: to help me become a person beyond how society sees me, labels me, and treats me. You look at me, overflowing with possibilities, even when I feel most limited and boxed into a tall story about who I am not.

I wouldn't have known the world I know now without you in it. It has become one of the safest places, where I feel heard and seen. You show up even when I don't need you the most and when I need you the most. And I realize it's always been you. Regardless of how many times love has fallen short, how years and distance have made me feel aggrieved at love, at you; I understand love goes through complex ways until you make it simple. Until loving again feels as easy as falling into a safety net.

- Inspired by the movie *Where the Crawdads Sing* (2022), directed by Olivia Newman.

Someone Who Sits Through the Storms

Can we talk about Marisol's role in *A Man Called Otto*?

She's a new neighbor, and to me, she's sent as "something" to Otto's life. Someone who breaks the walls for a reason. Someone who pulls a knot close to make Otto feel he's not alone in his grief, longing, and shadowed reflections. That there's someone willing to sit down with him and listen to his heart's bare tones without judgment. That there's a space for him where he is heard and understood—only if he allows himself to pour out his truth, however disturbing and uncomfortable; only if he allows someone in not to ease the storms but to be simply with him until the storms ease.

The biggest takeaway I had was that no one knows what someone goes through behind closed doors: someone's loss, burdens, or unhealed wounds. No one knows the unspeakable, and that's when we most need to be gentle. To speak aloud the language of kindness. I hope we all make a difference in someone's life this way.

- Inspired by the movie *A Man Called Otto (2022),* directed by Marc Forster.

The Language of Places

For some, it may be the most underrated gesture to show someone places, but I find it a language that means uncovering oneself to someone dearly valued. I think of a place as a book that bears the geography of a person, with all its mountains and crevices; when someone says, "I'll show you Sicily," or Florence, or the Uffizi Gallery, or some place you've never been, it sometimes means, "I'll show you myself."

Being shown places is also like being shown the kind of person you are with. You realize you don't fully know the person and that there are still places you haven't stepped into. And being invited in or allowed to enter means being shown pages beyond the physical and becoming an open book with you.

- Inspired by the mini-series *From Scratch (2022)*, directed by Nzingha Stewart & Dennie Gordon.

A Hundred Countries Away

Now that you're this close to me, I see more clearly how lacking my life has been after long years of not being with you. How sunsets sank in muted colors, as if there was no more life in them. How these fingers ached to entwine with yours, locking ourselves in our own world. But this vision of a world shared with you didn't grow bigger, as you needed to cross a newer distance with vague bridges that might never bring our paths together again.

I searched for you, and I might have felt hopeless about meeting you eye to eye again in a sea of strangers and in a city that doesn't know me, nor the language I speak. But today, there's hope—hope to see you again and spend brief moments with you in places we can't call our own. Perhaps this is why, even if you're near and within my reach, it still feels like you are a hundred countries away from me. And right there, I understand that even if I could talk to you inches away, in a language only we would understand, it still wouldn't change the fact that there's a new language you are more comfortable speaking now.

And I stutter when I try to speak it. I feel lost between the lines, and I always end up being inarticulate. This heart… it has always been eloquent around you. It speaks the language you speak, but it's never strong enough to cross the middle ground where we both can meet, sing it together, and stop being speechless.

- Inspired by the romantic drama *Past Lives (2023),* directed by Celine Song.

Currents of the Heart.

Teach Me Who I Am

I wanted you to be honest with me. Be open about what goes through your mind or what you want to say each time I unconsciously make you feel disrespected or unconsidered. You don't have to keep silent about it—teach me by letting me know what I have done wrong so I can correct myself. Teach me—because I know so little about myself. I don't see myself from the different angles that only you do, and there are words I don't realize are unkind enough to hurt you—let me know about the fault lines I make, the cuts I've caused, and where I hurt you the most.

As much as possible, I want you to be open with me by communicating how I make you feel. Teach me—because not all the time I know a lot about what I speak or do. And that is when I need you the most to remind me who I am.

Soft Entrances

I will always be that place you can come back to. I promise you this—do you still recall? I have never built taller walls or tightened my defenses since you left because I still wanted to be good to you, despite what you did. I will never hold grudges against you. I will never spray-paint your name all over my house to warn you that you are restricted from entering this place, that you don't belong here anymore.

I keep that promise to greet you with the same open hands, like nothing ever crashed down. Like I didn't lose the biggest part of me when you left. I don't want to punish myself by pressing all the memories of you into cigarette sticks and hurting my lungs every single day, or by clenching your name in my fist because that won't do to lighten the boulders.

Instead, I clear the air and soften all the possible entrances that could lead you back to me because I want you to arrive here, safe. Because I still love you. And I want you to believe that I'm still your safe place.

That here, I won't hurt you. Here, I won't ever do the same thing you did to me.

To Grieve on the Living

It's almost terrifying to look at you every day and think all the sides of you that I've grown familiar and comfortable with will fade one day. I think about it with fear at the back of my head when I'm happiest with you — the inevitability of you gone out of both sight and touch. It's what kills me every time I get to witness your presence and how you burst miracles in front of me knowing that you'll never sit in a beautiful place with me forever. That I can't always immerse myself in all the bright moments, or frolic under heavy skies with you. That time is something I can't compel to pause and go my way because just like you — it must pass.

And this is beyond my grip however I want time to linger more with us like an undying scent. Like a host of flowers that fills up the core of my skeleton. I understand time will always come to empty me and only leave me with breadcrumbs of you that remind me you were once here. That I once witnessed life as beautiful as yours here. That there was once a streak of hope through all the places you've touched with your presence. That there was once love and blessing that crossed my path when I was on the verge of losing faith that both are real.

If I could decide, I wouldn't want to lose sight of you. I wouldn't want to talk about how you slipped away because I don't think I could manage the cuts. I couldn't recount beautiful memories without pouring hard. I couldn't tone down the wounds when opening about you. I couldn't stop my heart from grieving at the thought of a future where you're no longer there to witness it with me.

But I'm glad I had the opportunity to meet you yesterday. I'm glad I still get to witness you today, even if it's uncertain you'll be present in all the tomorrows I'll live through next.

I'm glad because, at one point in my journey, there was a moment of magnificence when I crossed paths with you. And it aches to think that, just like all lives and other loves,

yours will also pass.

About the author

Admer Balingan

Admer is a freelance copywriter, editor, and a wanderer at heart. They revel in all things poetic, off-the-beaten-track, and fairy-witch-cottage-core.

They are the author of Metamorphosis, Fish Deprived, and Name Your Fist After Tenderness, along with several books they co-authored, including Magkasintahan, Ink Spilled in Autumn, and The Dark is Waiting to Sing. Their works have recently appeared on Spillwords.com.

They have also contributed to both local and international book anthologies and won Poet of the Year for their firstborn, Metamorphosis, during the Literary Awards 2022.

When not writing, they explore occult knowledge, read horoscopes, and binge-watch Schitt's Creek.

www.ingramcontent.com/pod-product-compliance
Lightning Source LLC
LaVergne TN
LVHW041552070526
838199LV00046B/1928